D0466209

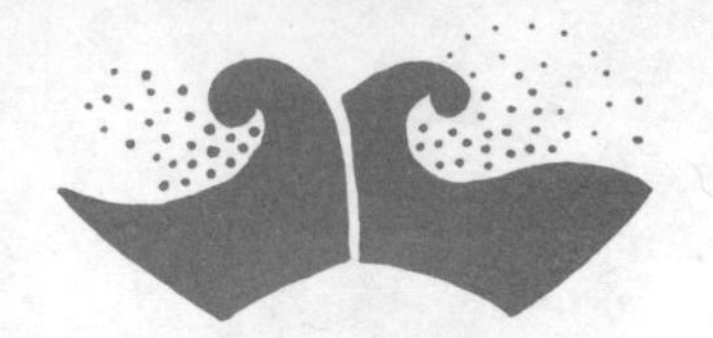

Grand Opening

February 11, 2000

Newport Public Library Foundation

The Strange and ROBERT

by Steven Bauer

illustrated by Brad Sneed

Wonderful Tale of McDOODLE

{The Boy Who Wanted to Be a Dog}

Simon & Schuster Books for Young Readers

SIMON & SCHUSTER BOOKS FOR YOUNG READERS
An imprint of Simon & Schuster Children's Publishing Division
1230 Avenue of the Americas, New York, New York 10020

Book design by Paul Zakris
The text for this book is set in 15-point Minion 578 Bold.
The illustrations are rendered in watercolor on 140-pound, cold-press watercolor paper.
Printed in Hong Kong
10 9 8 7 6 5 4 3 2 1

LIBRARY OF CONGRESS CATALOGING-IN-PUBLICATION DATA
Bauer, Steven.
The strange and wonderful tale of Robert McDoodle: the boy who wanted to be a dog / Steven Bauer ; illustrated by Brad Sneed.
p. cm.
Summary: Young Robert McDoodle thinks that his parents plan to give him a new shirt for his sixth birthday, so he decides to go to obedience school to learn how to be a dog.
ISBN 0-689-80619-1 (hardcover)
[1. Dogs—Fiction. 2. Stories in rhyme.] I. Sneed, Brad, ill.
II. Title.
PZ8.3.B325St 1999
[E]—dc20
96-35360
CIP AC

For Liz
—S. B.

To Garrett, Jolie and Sidney
—B. S.

Robert McDoodle was soon to be six,

and his parents were up to their usual tricks.

He'd found in the dustiness under their bed—

pink socks, a red shirt, and a new pair of Keds.

He groaned and he grumbled. How could they think
he wanted new sneakers, or anything pink?
For his birthday, a six-year-old (everyone knows)
doesn't want something as boring as clothes.

And anyway, Robert had plenty of *stuff*—
Nintendo, a skateboard, and comics enough
for a lifetime, a neat model train that could fly
round the loop-de-loop tracks in the wink of an eye.

What he wanted was nothing his parents could buy.

CANINES

Now, most boys will tell you that when they are grown
they want to go searching for dinosaur bones.
They'll say, if you ask, that just like their pops,
they want to be astronauts, lawyers, or cops.

But Robert was different, for when he grew up,

he wanted to be the World's First Human Pup.

The dogs on his street were the happiest bunch.

They never were called by their mothers for lunch.

They never wore jackets; they never wore shoes.

They never were forced to eat broccoli or stews,

or go to the dentist, sleep under a sheet.

They got to go outside in rainstorms and sleet.

The life of a dog—well, it couldn't be beat!

But he was a boy, and he knew, in September,
he'd go to a school where they'd make him remember
the names of the states, and their capitals, too,
the imports and exports of Spain and Peru.

He'd sit at a desk and have to be still
when he wanted to shout, or to tumble downhill.
Adding insult to injury, brickbat to hurt,
for his birthday his parents had bought him a shirt

when he'd much rather dig with the dogs in the dirt.

South America
Brazil's flag

His parents, quite clearly, were blind to his plight,
so he packed a small satchel and slipped out one night.
His plan was to hunt for a *dog* school, yes sir!
where he'd learn how to dig and perhaps grow some fur.

He asked all the kids that he met the next day,
but none of the boys or the girls knew the way.
He was hungry and hot; he'd about given up
when he suddenly realized he should have asked *pups*.

Sure enough, in a twinkling, a malamute told him
about an obedience class that might hold him.
The school's name was Jellicoe, built near a bog
that was filled every night with the twanging of frogs—

There a boy might be taught how to act like a dog.

The teacher was four-pawed, with sharp shiny biters,
and muscles enough for a ring full of fighters.
Her growl was ferocious, her bark sharp as glass—
a large German shepherd, her nickname was Cass.

"You're an odd-looking dog," she told Robert McDoodle.
"Are you some kind of furless and newfangled poodle?"
"No," Robert told her. "I'm merely a squirt
who came here to learn how to dig in the dirt."

"We'll see about that," Cass said with a bark.
"You think that the life of a dog is a lark?
Guarding lessons at one; Speech at two on the dot.
We'll fit you in Class Number Three's vacant slot.

"But your name can't be Robert. It has to be Spot."

The first day was harder than Spot had supposed.
His practice at Sniffing got grass up his nose.
The sides of his mouth ached from Holding a Stick,
and he pulled from his arm what he thought was a tick.

The next day was Panting, and Drinking from Bowls,
and Pushing Your Muzzle Deep into Holes.
He found out how Nipping at Fur bit off fleas,
while Nipping at Haunches was mainly to tease.

He hadn't known dogs lapped up water from toilets—
he hoped that the *least* they had done was to boil it!
By the end of a week, Robert had to admit
that at one or two moments he'd wanted to quit.

There was more to a dog than he'd known—quite a bit.

Aside from the basics like Barking at Squirrels

and Jumping (with Mud) on the Clean Skirts of Girls,

he'd had to learn Scratching, which went on for minutes,

and Pawing a Hole, when a snake was still in it!

He'd had to learn Staying, which just drove him crazy;

he might as well sit at a desk and be lazy!

In addition to this, there was Snapping at Flies,

and Rolling on Dead Things, and Howling at Skies,

And Making a Tour of the Entire Yard,

and Marking, which certainly didn't *look* hard.

However, if you have just two legs, not four,

then Marking can make you land right on the floor—

Spot knew; he had practiced until he was sore.

On top of all that, he'd learned digging by then,
and been floored to discover that something like ten
types of digging existed, and he was a witness:
There was (1) Digging for Cardiovascular Fitness,

(2) Digging for Groundhogs and (3) Woodchucks and (4) Moles,
and (5) Just for the Pleasure of Making New Holes.
There was (6) Digging to Find What the Last Dog Had Hidden,
and (7) Digging in Flower Beds—Strictly Forbidden!

There was (8) Digging for Insects and Earthworms and Grubs,
and a rigorous project called (9) Uprooting Shrubs.
And last but not least, there was (10) Scraping the Ground
in Order to Bury the Bone You Had Found,

Accomplished (of course) Without Making a Sound.

SPOT
DOZER
FLAPS

One night, when the kennel was quiet and dark,
and stars through the fence looked like smoldering sparks,
Robert rested, dog-tired, and started to doubt
that his eager ambition would somehow work out.

Next week was his birthday, and what could he do?
If he were a dog, he would be *forty-two,*
for he had just learned that a dog ages seven
long years for each one that a human is given.

He was too young for that! He was really just *six!*
He suddenly yearned for his parents' old tricks.
They might not be dogs, but they *were* his own kind.
Sad but resolved, Robert made up his mind

to soon leave the Jellicoe Dog School behind.

The day of his birthday was blue-skied and sunny
and Robert McDoodle considered it funny
that none of the dogs he had romped with each day
could be seen from the oak under which he now lay.

"Where have they gone to? Where can they be?"
he asked as he scraped the dirt under the tree.
When Cassie suggested they trot to the field,
Robert followed beside her; he actually heeled.

They rounded a corner and mounted a rise . . .

. . . when all of the dogs from the school barked,

"SURPRISE!"

Robert couldn't believe it. They'd managed to fool
the most human doggie who went to their school.
"And now for your pleasure," Cass said with a shout,
at which Robert's mother and father burst out.

"*There* you are!" said his father. "You think you're a smarty.
You thought you could get out of having a party?"
They had kibble and biscuits down by the lake
and a big lie-down dinner of liver and steak,

and for Robert a huge bowl of ice cream and cake.

"Good-bye!" all the dogs howled as he drove away.
Robert's parents had promised he'd come back to play.
He lay on the backseat and smiled at his lap
where a floppy-eared basset hound puppy now sat.

"Happy Birthday!" his mom said. "Hurrah!" said his dad.
Robert thought that his parents weren't really so bad.
It was fun to be sitting behind them this way
as they drove straight for home on this beautiful day.

He felt that a bed would be nice for a change,
and not having to fret about fleas or the mange.
He remembered his neighborhood, kit and caboodle,
his favorite dinner of Szechwan noodles.

It was really quite great to be Robert McDoodle!